I0817754

BISON
BOOKS

Bess Streeter Aldrich

Journey into Christmas

and

Star across the Tracks

University of Nebraska Press
Lincoln

"Journey into Christmas" and "Star across the Tracks" were previously published in *Journey into Christmas and Other Stories* (New York: Appleton-Century-Crofts, Inc., 1949). First Nebraska printing 1985. Reprinted by arrangement with E. P. Dutton, Inc.
 Manufactured in the United States of America.

The University of Nebraska Press is part of a land-grant institution with campuses and programs on the past, present, and future homelands of the Pawnee, Ponca, Otoe-Missouria, Omaha, Dakota, Lakota, Kaw, Cheyenne, and Arapaho Peoples, as well as those of the relocated Ho-Chunk, Sac and Fox, and Iowa Peoples.

Library of Congress Cataloging-in-Publication Data
Names: Aldrich, Bess Streeter, 1881–1954, author. | Aldrich, Bess Streeter, 1881–1954. Journey into Christmas. | Aldrich, Bess Streeter, 1881–1954. Star across the tracks.
Title: Journey into Christmas and Star across the tracks / Bess Streeter Aldrich.
Other titles: Journey into Christmas (Compilation) | Star across the tracks.
Description: Lincoln : University of Nebraska Press, 2022.
Identifiers: LCCN 2022008534
ISBN 9781496233042 (paperback)
Subjects: LCSH: Christmas stories, American. | BISAC: FICTION / Short Stories (single author) | FICTION / Holidays |
LCGFT: Christmas fiction. | Short stories.
Classification: LCC PS3501.L378 J683 2022 |
DDC 813/.52—dc23/eng/20220310
LC record available at https://lccn.loc.gov/2022008534

Set in Linotype New Caledonia by Laura Buis.

Illustrations on pages 9 and 38 are by James Aldrich.

Contents

Journey into Christmas

and

Star across the Tracks

Journey into Christmas

MARGARET STALEY STOOD at her library window looking out at the familiar elms and the lace-vine arbor. Tonight the trees were snow-crusted, the arbor a thing of crystal filigree under the Christmas stars.

Some years the Midwest stayed mild all through December, donning its snowsuit only after the holidays. But tonight was a Christmas Eve made to order, as though Nature had supervised the designing and decorating of a silvered stage setting.

Margaret Staley visualized all this perfection, but she knew that the very beauty of the scene brought into sharper contrast the fact that for the first time in her life she was alone on Christmas Eve.

For fifty-nine Christmases she had been surrounded by the people she loved. On this sixtieth, there was no one. For not one of her four children was coming home.

She could remember reading a story like that once, about a mother who was disappointed that no one was coming—and then, just at dusk on Christmas Eve, all the children and their families arrived together to surprise her. But that was a sentimental piece of fiction; this was cold reality.

The reasons for none of the four coming were all good. Three of the reasons were, anyway, she admitted reluctantly. Calling the roll she went over—for the hundredth time—why each could not make the trip.

Don. That was understandable. Don and Janet, his wife, and young Ralph in California could not be expected to come half way across the continent every year, and they had been here last Christmas. She herself had visited them the past summer, returning as late as September.

Ruth. Ruth was her career daughter, connected with a children's hospital and vitally important to her post. Long ago she had accepted the fact that Ruth could give her only the fragments from a busy life and never had she begrudged it; indeed, she had felt vicariously a part of her capable daughter's service to humanity.

Jean. Jeanie and her husband, Roy, lived in Chicago. Jeanie was a great family girl and certainly would have come out home, but the two little boys were in quarantine.

Lee. The hurt which she had loyally pushed into the back of her mind jumped out again like an unwanted and willful jack-in-the-box. Lee and his Ann could have come. Living in Oklahoma, not too far away, they could have made the trip if they had wished. Or if it had not been convenient for Lee to leave, she could have gone down there to be with them. *If they had asked her.*

The only time Christmas had been mentioned was in a letter, now several weeks old. Lee had mentioned casually that they were going to have company for Christmas. That would be Ann's folks of course. You mustn't be selfish. You had to remember that there were in-laws to be taken into consideration.

Standing there at the window, looking out at the silver night, she remembered how she once thought the family would always come home. In her younger years she had said complacently, "I know my children. They love their old home and whenever possible they will spend Christmas in it. Of course there will be sickness and other reasons to keep them away at times, but some of the four will always be here." And surprisingly it had been true. Someone had been here every Christmas.

Faintly into her reveries came the far-off sound of bells and she opened the casement window a bit to locate their tinkling. It was the carolers, carrying out the town's traditional singing on Christmas Eve.

She closed the window and drew the drapes, as though unable to bear the night's white beauty and the poignant notes of young voices.

"I'm alone . . . I'm alone . . . it's Christmas Eve and I'm alone." Her mind repeated it like some mournful raven with its "nevermore."

Suddenly she caught herself by a figurative grip. "Now, listen," she said to that self which was grieving. "You are not a weak person and you're not neurotic. You have good sense and understanding and even humor at times. How often have you criticized people for this very thing?"

She walked over to the radio and turned it on, but when "*Silent Night . . . Holy Night*" came softly forth, she snapped it off, afraid she would break down and weep like an old Niobe.

"Oh, go on . . . feel sorry for yourself if you want to. Go on. Do it." She smiled again wryly, and knew she was trying to clutch at humor, that straw which more than once had saved her from drowning in troubled waters.

She went over to her desk and got out the four last letters from the children, although she knew their contents thoroughly.

There was the fat one from Don and Janet with young Ralph's hastily scribbled sixth-grade enclosure. They said the poinsettias were up to the back porch roof, that the Christmas parade had been spectacular, and that they would all be thinking of her on Christmas day when they drove to Laguna Beach.

Then the letter from Jeanie. She had been experiencing one of those times which mothers have to expect, but they were over the hump now and although still in quarantine, she thought Bud could be dressed and Larry sit up by Christmas day. They would all miss the annual trip out home but would be thinking of her.

Ruth's letter was a series of disconnected notes written in odd moments at her desk. Almost one could catch a whiff of hospital odors from them. They were filled with plans for the nurses, the carols, the trees for the convalescents, but as always she would think, too, of home and mother on Christmas day.

From Lee and Ann, nothing but that three-, no, *four*-weeks-old letter with its single casual reference to Christmas. There was a package from them under the tree, attractively packed and addressed in Ann's handwriting. It, too, had been here for weeks. But no recent letter. No special. No wire. No "We will be thinking of you" as the others had written. She tried to push the hurt back and close the lid on it, but she could not forget it was there.

She put the letters away and went into the living room. It looked as big as Grand Central Station. Last year there had been eleven sitting in these chairs which tonight were as empty as her heart. Half ashamed at her childishness in trying to create an illusion, she began pulling them out to form the semicircle of last year when the big tree had been its pivotal point. She could even recall where each had sat that morning at the opening of the gifts. Jeanie and Bud on the davenport, Ruth curled up on the hassock, Ann and Lee side by side in the big blue chairs—and on around the circle.

She had to smile again to remember the red rocking-chair which she brought from the storeroom for young Larry. It had been her own little rocker and was fifty-eight years old. A brown tidy hung limply on its cane back, an old-fashioned piece worked in cross-stitch, the faded red letters reading: FOR MARGARET. Larry had squeezed into it, but when his name was called and he rose excitedly to get his first present, the chair rose with him and they had to pry him out of it and one of the chair's arms cracked. There had been so much hilarious laughter where tonight was only silence. And silence can be so very much louder than noise.

With the chairs forming their ghost-like semicircle behind her, she turned her own around to the fireplace and sat down to give herself the pleasure and the pain of remembering old Christmases. Swiftly her mind traversed the years, darting from one long gone holiday season to another.

The Christmas before Don was born she and John were in their first new home. They had been very happy that year, just the two of them; so happy in fact that she had felt almost conscience

stricken to think she could be contented without her own old family at holiday time. Why, she thought suddenly, that was the way Lee was feeling now, and she could not help a twinge of jealousy at the parting of the ways.

Then Don's first Christmas when he was eleven months old. After these thirty-six years she could still remember how he clutched a big glass marble and would not notice anything else. Strange how much small details stayed in one's mind.

The Christmas before Jeanie was born, when she did not go out to shop, but sent for her gifts by mail, so that the opening of them was almost as much a surprise to her as to the recipients.

Then there was the whooping-cough Christmas, with the house full of medicated steam and all four youngsters dancing and whooping spasmodically around the tree like so many little Indians.

There was the time she bought the big doll for Ruth and when it proved to have a large paint blemish on its leg, she wanted to return it for a perfect one. But Ruth would not hear of it and made neat little bandages for the leg as though it were a wound. It was the first she ever noticed Ruth's nursing instincts.

Dozens of memories flocked to her mind. There had not always been happy holidays. Some of them were immeasurably sad. Darkest of all was the one after John's death, with the children trying to carry out cheerfully the old family customs, knowing that it was what Dad would have wanted. But even in the troubled days there had been warm companionship to share the burden—not this icy loneliness.

For a few moments she sat, unmoving, lost in the memory of that time, then roused herself to continue her mental journeying.

Soon after that dark one, Christmas was no longer a childish affair. Gifts suddenly ceased to be skates and hockey-sticks and became sorority party dresses and fraternity rings, and the house was full of young people home for vacation. Then the first marriage and Don's Janet was added to the circle, then Jeanie brought Roy into it. In time the first grandson . . . and another . . . and a third—all the youthful pleasure of the older members of the family renewed through the children's eyes.

Then came that Christmas when the blast of the ships in their harbor had sent its detonations here into this very living room, as into every one in the country. And though all were here and tried to be natural and merry, only the children were free from forebodings of what the next year would bring. And it brought many changes: Don with his Reserves, Roy enlisting in the Navy, Lee in the Army. That was the year they expected Lee home from the nearby camp. His presents were under the tree and the Christmas Eve dinner ready, only to have him phone that his leave had been canceled, so that the disappointment was keener than if they had not expected him at all.

Then those dark holiday times with all three boys overseas and Jean and the babies living here at home. Ruth in uniform, coming for one Christmas, calm and clear-eyed as always, realizing perhaps more than the others that at home or abroad, walking or sleeping, Death holds us always in the hollow of his hand.

Then the clouds beginning to lift and, one by one, all coming back, Lee the last to arrive. And that grand reunion of last year after all the separations and the fears. All safe. All home. The warm touch of the hand and the welcoming embrace. Pretty Ann added to the circle. The decorating of the tree. The lights in the window. The darting in and out for last minute gift wrapping. The favorite recipes. Old songs resung. Old family jokes retold. Old laughter renewed. In joy and humility she had said, "My cup runneth over."

Recalling all this, she again grew stern with herself. How could one ask for anything more after that safe return and perfect reunion? But the contrast between then and tonight was too great. All her hopes had ended in loneliness. All her fears of approaching age had become true. One could not help the deep depression. The head may tell the heart all sorts of sensible things, but at Christmastime the heart is stronger.

She sat for a long time in front of the fire which had not warmed her. She had been on a long emotional journey and it had left her tired and spent.

From the library, loud and brazen, the phone rang. It startled her for she had never outgrown her fear of a late call. With her usual trepidation she hastened to answer. There was some delay, a far off operator's voice, and then Lee.

"That you, Mother?"

"Yes, Lee, yes. How are you?"

"Fine. Did Jeanie come?"

"No, the boys are still quarantined."

"Ruth?"

"No."

"You there alone?"

"Yes."

"Gosh, that's too bad on the old family night. Well, cheer up. I've got news for you. Our company came. She weighs seven pounds and fourteen ounces."

"What . . . what did you say, Lee?"

"Our daughter arrived, Mom. Four hours ago. I waited at the hospital to see that Ann was all right."

"Why, Lee . . . you never told . . . we never knew . . ."

"It was Ann's idea of a good joke. And listen . . . we named her Margaret . . . for you, Mother. Do you like it?"

"Why, yes . . . *yes*, I *do* like it, Lee."

There was more, sometimes both talking at once and having to repeat. Then Lee saying, "We were wondering if you could come down in a couple of weeks. Ann thinks she'd like to have an old hand at the business around. Can you arrange it?"

"Oh, yes, Lee . . . I'm sure I could."

"Good. Well, I'll hang up now. Spent enough on my call . . . have to save money to send Margaret to college. Be seeing you."

"*Lee* . . ." In those last seconds she wanted desperately to put into words all the things her heart was saying. But you cannot put the thoughts garnered from a life of love and service into a sentence. So she only said: "Be a good dad, Lee. Be as good a dad as . . ." She broke off, but he understood.

"I know . . . I'll try. Merry Christmas, Mom."

"Merry Christmas, Lee."

She put down the receiver and walked into the living room, walked briskly as though to tell her news, her heart beating with pleasant excitement. The semicircle of chairs confronted her. With physical sight she saw their emptiness. But, born of love and imagination, they were all occupied as plainly as ever eyes had seen them. She had a warm sense of companionship. The house seemed alive with humans. How could they be so real? She swept the circle with that second sight which had been given her. Don over there . . . Ruth on the hassock . . . Jeanie on the davenport . . . Lee and Ann in the big blue chairs . . .

Suddenly she turned and walked hurriedly down the hall to the closet and came back with the little red chair. She pushed the two blue chairs apart and set the battered rocker between them. On the back hung the old brown tidy with its red cross-stitching: FOR MARGARET.

She smiled at it happily. All her numbness of spirit had vanished, her loneliness gone. This was a good Christmas. Why, this was one of the best Christmases she ever had!

She felt a sudden desire to go back to the library, to look out at the silvery garden and up to the stars. That bright one up there—it must be the one that stops over all cradles . . .

Faintly she could hear bells and voices. That would be the young crowd coming back from their caroling, so she opened the window again.

Oh, little town of Bethlehem,
How still we see thee lie . . .

The words came clearly across the starlit snow, singing themselves into her consciousness with a personal message:

Yet in thy dark streets shineth
The everlasting light
The hopes and fears of all the years
Are met in thee tonight.

The hopes and fears of all the years! She felt the old Christmas lift of the heart, that thankfulness and joy she had always experienced when the children were all together . . . all well . . . all home.

"My cup runneth over."

At the door of the living room she paused to turn off the lights. Without looking toward the circle of chairs, so there might come no disillusion, she said over her shoulder:

"Good-night children, Merry Christmas. See you early in the morning."

Star across the Tracks

MR. HARM KURTZ sat in the kitchen with his feet in the oven and discussed the world; that is to say, his own small world. His audience, shifting back and forth between the pantry and the kitchen sink, caused the orator's voice to rise and fall with its coming and going.

The audience was mamma. She was the bell upon which the clapper of his verbal output always struck. As she never stopped moving about at her housework during these nightly discourses, one might have said facetiously that she was his Roaming Forum.

Pa Kurtz was slight and wiry, all muscle and bounce. His wife had avoirdupois to spare and her leisurely walk was what is known in common parlance as a waddle. She wore her hair combed high, brushed tightly up at the back and sides, where it ended in a hard knot on the top of her head. When movie stars and café society took it up, mamma said she had beat them to it by thirty-five years.

The Kurtzes lived in a little brown house on Mill Street, which meandered its unpaved way along a creek bed. The town, having been laid out by the founding fathers on this once-flowing but now long-dried creek, was called River City.

For three days of his working week pa's narrow world held sundry tasks: plowing gardens, cutting alfalfa, hauling lumber from the mill. For the other three days he was engaged permanently as a handyman by the families of Scott, Dillingham and Porter, who lived on High View Drive, far away from Mill Street, geographically, economically, socially. And what mamma hadn't learned about the Scott, Dillingham and Porter domestic establishments in the last few years wasn't worth knowing.

Early in his labors for the three families, pa had summed them up to mamma in one sweeping statement: "The Scotts . . . him I like and her I don't like. The Dillinghams . . . her I like and him I don't. The Porters . . . both I don't like."

The Porters' house was brick colonial. The Scotts' was a rambling stone of the ranch type. The Dillinghams' had no classification, but was both brick and stone, to say nothing of stained shingles, lumber, tile, glass bricks and stucco.

The Porters had four children of school age. Also they had long curving rows of evergreens in which the grackles settled with raucous glee as though to outvie the family's noise. The grackles—and for all pa knew, maybe the young folks also—drove Mrs. Porter wild, but pa rather liked the birds. They sounded so countrylike, and he had never grown away from the farm.

Mr. Porter was a lawyer and a councilman. Mrs. Porter was a member of the Garden Club and knew practically all there was to know about flora and fauna. She went in for formal beds of flowers, rectangles and half-moons, containing tulips and daffodils in the spring and dahlias and asters later. She ruled pa with iron efficiency. With a wave of her hand she might say: "Mr. Kurtz, I think I'll have the beds farther apart this year."

And pa, telling mamma about it at night, would sneer: "Just like they was the springs-and-mattress kind you can shove around on casters."

Mrs. Scott went to the other extreme. She knew the least about vegetation of anyone who had ever come under pa's scrutiny. Assuredly he was his own boss there. Each spring she tossed him several dozen packages of seeds as though she dared him to do his worst. Once he had found rutabaga and spinach among the packages of zinnias and nasturtiums. But pa couldn't be too hard on her, for she had a little cripple son who took most of her time. And he liked the fresh-colored packages every year and the feel of the warm moist earth when he put in the seeds. The head of the house was a doctor and if he happened to drive in while pa was there, he stopped and joked a bit.

The Dillinghams' yard was pa's favorite. The back of it was not only informal, it was woodsy. Mrs. Dillingham told pa she had been raised on a farm and that the end of the yard reminded her of the grove back of her old home. She had no children and often she came out to stand around talking to pa or brought her gloves and worked with him.

"Poor thing! Lonesome," mamma said at once when he was telling her.

Mrs. Dillingham had pa set out wild crab apple and ferns and plum trees, little crooked ones, so it would "look natural." Several times she had driven him out to the country and they had brought back shooting stars and swamp candle, Dutchman's-breeches and wood violets. Pa's hand with the little wild flowers was as tender as the hand of God.

When Mr. Dillingham came home from his big department store, he was loud and officious, sometimes critical of what had been done.

In winter, the work for the High View homes was just as hard and far less interesting. Storm windows, snow on long driveways, basements to be cleaned. It was always good to get home and sit with his tired, wet feet in the oven and tell the day's experiences to mamma. There was something very comforting about mamma, her consoling "Oh, think nothing of it," or her sympathetic clucking of "Tsk . . . tsk . . . them women, with their cars and their clubs!"

Tonight there was more than usual to tell, for there had been great goings on up in High View. Tomorrow night was Christmas Eve and in preparation for the annual prizes given by the federated civic clubs, his three families had gone in for elaborate outdoor decorations.

There was unspoken rivalry among the three houses too. Pa could sense it. Mrs. Porter had asked him offhandedly, as though it were a matter of extreme unconcern, what the two other families were planning to do. And Mr. Dillingham had asked the same thing, but bluntly. You couldn't catch pa that way, though, he reminded mamma with great glee. "Slippery as a eel!" Had just answered that the others seemed to be hitchin' up a lot of wiring.

But pa had known all along what each one was doing. And tomorrow night everybody would know. The Porters had long strings of blue lights which they were carrying out into the evergreens, as though bluebirds, instead of black ones, were settling there to stay through Christmas.

The Dillinghams had gone in for reindeer. They had ordered them made from plyboard at the mill, and tonight the eight deer, with artificial snow all over them, were prancing up the porch steps, while a searchlight on the ground threw the group into relief.

The Scotts, whose house was not so high as the others, had a fat Santa on the roof with one foot in the chimney. In a near-by dormer window there was a phonograph which would play Jingle Bells, so that the song seemingly came from the old fellow himself. It had made the little cripple boy laugh and clap his hands when they wheeled him outside to see the finished scene.

All this and much more pa was telling mamma while she ambled about, getting supper on the table.

Lillie came home. Lillie was the youngest of their three children and she worked for the Dillinghams, too, but in the department store. Lillie was a whiz with a needle, and a humble helper in the remodeling room. She made her own dresses at home and tried them on Maisie, the manikin. That was one of the store's moronic-looking models which had lost an arm and sundry other features, and Lillie had asked for it when she found they were going to discard it. Ernie, her brother, had brought it home in his car and repaired it. Now she hung her own skirts on Maisie to get their length. That was about all the good the manikin did her, for Lillie's circumference was fully three times that of the model.

The three of them sat down to eat, as Ernie would not arrive for a long time and mamma would warm things over for him. As usual, the table talk came largely from pa. He had to tell it all over to Lillie: the blue lights, the reindeer, the Santa-with-one-foot-in-the-chimney.

Lillie, who was a bit fed up with the paste-board reindeer and synthetic Santas at the store, thought she still would like to see them. So pa said tomorrow night after Carrie got here they would all drive to High View, that he himself would like to see them once from the paved street instead of with his head caught in an evergreen branch or getting a crick in his neck under a reindeer's belly.

They discussed the coming of the older daughter and her husband, Bert, and the two little boys, who were driving here from their home in another county and planning to stay two whole nights. A big event was Christmas this year in the Mill Street Kurtz house.

After supper when Lillie started the dishes, pa went out to see to the team and mamma followed to pick out two of her fat hens for the Christmas dinner.

In the dusk of the unusually mild December evening, mamma stood looking about her as with the eye of a stranger. Then she said she wished things had been in better shape before Carrie and Bert got here, that not one thing had been done around the place to fix it up since the last time.

"That rickety old shed, pa," she said mildly. "I remember as well as I'm standin' here you tellin' Carrie you was goin' to have that good new lumber on by the next time she come."

It was as match to pine shavings. It made pa good and mad. With him working his head off, day and night! He blew up. In anyone under twelve it would have been called a tantrum. He rushed over to the tool house and got his hammer and started to yank off a rotten board.

"I'll get this done before Carrie comes," he shouted, "if it's the last thing I do."

A psychoanalyst, after much probing, might have discovered what caused pa's sudden anger. But mamma, who knew less than nothing about psychoanalysis, having only good common sense, also knew what caused it.

Pa's own regrets over his big mistake made him irritable at times. He was one of those farmers who had turned their backs on old home places during the protracted drought. Mamma had wanted to stick it out another year, but he had said no, they would move to town where everybody earned good money. So they had sold the farm and bought this little place on Mill Street, the only section of town where one could keep a cow and chickens. The very next year crops were good again and now the man who had bought the old place for so little came to River City in a car as fine as the Dillinghams'. Yes, any casual criticism of the Mill Street place always touched him in a vital spot of his being. So he yanked and swore and jawed, more mad than ever that mamma had walked away and was not hearing him.

It was not hard to get the old boards off. Soon they lay on the ground in a scattered heap of rotting timbers. Bird and Bell, from their exposed position across the manger, snatched at the alfalfa hay, quivered their nostrils and looked disdainfully at proceedings. The cow chewed her cud in the loose-jawed way of cows and stared disinterestedly into space.

Looking at the animals of which he was so fond, pa admitted to himself he needn't have ripped the boards off until morning, but balmy weather was predicted all throughout Christmas. And mamma had made him pretty mad. Suddenly the fire of his anger went out, for he was remembering something Ernie had said and it tickled his fancy. The last time Carrie brought her little boys home, Ernie had told them it was bubble gum the cow was chewing and the kids had hung over the half door an hour or more waiting for the big bubble to blow out. Tomorrow night the little kids would be here and the thought of it righted the world again.

Mamma came toward him with two hens under her arms as though she wanted him to make up with her. But he fussed around among the boards, not wanting to seem pleasant too suddenly.

His flashlight lay on the ground, highlighting the open shed, and the street light, too, shone in. An old hen flew squawking out of the hay and the pigeons swooped down from the roof.

Mamma stood looking at it for quite a while, then all at once she chucked the hens under a box and hurried into the house. When she came out, she held Maisie, the manikin, in front of her and Lillie was close behind with her arms full of sheets.

"What you think you're up to?" pa asked.

"You let me be," mamma said pointedly. "I know what I'm doin'."

She set up the manikin and with deft touches Lillie draped the sheets over its body and head and arranged it so it was leaning over the manger. Then mamma put pa's flashlight down in the manger itself and a faint light shone through the cracks of the old boards.

"There!" said mamma, stepping back. "Don't that look for all the world like the Bible story?"

"Seems like it's makin' light of it," pa said critically. "The Scotts and the Dillinghams didn't do nothin' like that. They just used Santy Clauses."

"I ain't doin' it for show, like them," mamma retorted. "I'm doin' it for Carrie's little boys. Somethin' they can see for themselves when they drive in. Somethin' they'll never forget, like's not, as long as they live."

Mamma and Lillie went out to the fence to survey their handiwork from that point. They were standing there when Ernie drove into the yard. Ernie worked for the River City Body and Fender Wreck Company, and one viewing the car and hearing its noisy approach would have questioned whether he ever patronized his own company.

They were anxious to know what Ernie thought. There were the horses nuzzling the alfalfa, the cow chewing away placidly, and the pigeons on the ridgepole. And there was the white-robed figure bending over the faint glow in the manger.

Ernie stood without words. Then he said "For gosh sakes! What in time?" The words were crude, but the tone was reverent.

"Mamma did it for the kids," Lillie said. "She wants you to fix a star up over the stable. Mrs. Dillingham gave an old one to pa."

Ernie had been a fixer ever since he was a little boy. Not for his looks had the River City Body and Fender Works Company hired Ernie Kurtz. So after his warmed-over supper he got his tools and a coil of wire and fixed the yellow bauble high over the stable, the wire and the slim rod almost invisible, so that it seemed a star hung there by itself.

All the next day pa worked up on High View Drive and all day mamma cleaned the house, made doughnuts and cookies with green sugar on them, and dressed the fat hens, stuffing them to the bursting point with onion dressing.

Almost before they knew it, Christmas Eve had arrived, and Carrie and Bert and the two little boys were driving into the yard with everyone hurrying out to greet them.

"Why, mamma," Carrie said. "That old shed . . . it just gave me a turn when we drove in."

But mamma was a bit disappointed over the little boys. The older one comprehended what it meant and was duly awe-struck, but the younger one ran over to the manger and said: "When's she goin' to blow out her bubble gum?"

After they had taken in the wrapped presents and the mince pies Carrie had baked, pa told them how they were all going to drive up to High View and see the expensive decorations, stressing his own part in their preparation so much that mamma said, "Don't brag. A few others had somethin' to do with it, you know." And Ernie sent them all into laughter when he called it High Brow Drive.

Then he went after his girl, Annie Hansen, and when they came back, surprisingly her brother was with them, which sent Lillie into a state of fluttering excitement.

So they all started out in two cars. Ernie and his girl and Lillie in Ernie's one seat, with the brother in the back, his long legs dangling out. Carrie and Bert took their little boys and mamma and pa. Not knowing the streets leading to the winding High View section, Bert stayed close behind Ernie's car, which chugged its way ahead of them like a noisy tugboat.

Everyone was hilariously happy. As for pa, his anger about mamma's chidings was long forgotten. All three of his children home and the two little kids. The Dillinghams didn't have any children at all for Christmas fun. *We never lost a child*, he was thinking, *and the Porters lost that little girl. Our grandkids tough as tripe, and the Scotts got that cripple boy*. It gave him a light-hearted feeling of freedom from disaster. Now this nice sightseeing trip in Bert's good car. Home to coffee and doughnuts, with the kids hanging up their stockings. Tomorrow the presents and a chicken dinner. For fleeting moments Pa Kurtz had a warm little-boy feeling of his own toward Christmas.

Mamma, too, said she hadn't had such a good time since Tige was a pup. And when one of the little boys said he wanted to see Tige when they got back, everyone laughed immoderately.

They passed decorated houses and countless trees brightly lighted in windows. Then around the curving streets of the High View district, following Ernie's noisy lead so closely that Carrie said they were just like Mary's little lamb. Across the street from the Porters' colonial house, Ernie stopped, and they stopped too.

The evergreens with their sparkling blue lights seemed a part of an enchanted forest. Carrie said she never saw anything so pretty in her life and waxed so enthusiastic that pa reminded her again of his big part in it.

When Ernie yelled back to ask if they'd seen enough, pa waved him on. And around the curve they went to the Dillinghams'.

There were other cars in front of the houses. Pa said like as not the judges themselves were right now deciding the prizes, and by the tone of his voice one would have thought the fate of the nation hung on the decision.

At the Dillinghams', the little boys waxed more excited over the reindeer, lighted by the search-light which threw them into snow-white relief. Yes, pa said, it was worth all the work they'd put on them.

Then to Doctor Scott's, and here the little boys practically turned inside out. For Santa himself was up on the roof as plain as day; and more, he was singing "Jingle bells . . . jingle bells." When he stopped, they clapped their hands and yelled up at him: "Hi, Santy! Sing more." And the adults all clapped too.

Then Ernie signaled and the little procession swung down out of High View and circled into the part of town where the blocks were prosaically rectangular and everything became smaller; yards, houses, Christmas trees.

"Look!" mamma said happily. "Ain't it nice? There ain't no patent on it. Everyone can make merry. Every little house can have its own fun and tree, just the same as the big ones."

Over the railroad tracks they went and into Mill Street, where Ernie adroitly picked his way around the mushy spots in the unpaved road, with Bert following his zigzag lead. And the trip was over.

There were Bird and Bell and the cow. There were the pigeons huddled together on the stable roof. There were the white Mary and the light in the manger, and the star. The laughter died down. Everyone got out quietly. Carrie ran her arm through her mother's. "I like yours, too, mamma," she said.

Inside, they grew merry again. Over the coffee and the doughnuts and sandwiches there was a lot

of talk. They argued noisily about the prize places for the decorated houses, betting one another which ones would win. Carrie and Lillie both thought the lights in the trees were by far the most artistic. Ma and Ernie's girl were for the reindeer at Dillinghams'. But Lillie's potential beau and Ernie and Bert and the little boys were all for the Scotts' Santa Claus. Pa, as one who had been the creator of them all, stayed benignly neutral.

After a while Ernie took his girl home. Her brother stood around on the porch awhile with Lillie and then left. The little boys hung up their stockings, with the grown folks teasing them, saying Santy could never find his way from the Scotts' down those winding streets.

Mamma and pa kept their own bedroom. Lillie took Carrie in with her. Bert went up to the attic with Ernie. Mamma made the little boys a bed on the couch, with three chairs in front to keep them from falling out. She had no sheets left for them, but plenty of clean patchwork quilts.

In the morning there were the sketchy breakfast and the presents, including a dishpan for mamma, who had never had a new one since her wedding day; the bit and braces pa had wished for so long; a flowered comb-and-brush set for Lillie; and fully one-third of the things for which the little boys had wished.

The children could play with their new toys and the men pitch horseshoes, but mamma and the girls had to hop right into the big dinner, for everyone would be starved. Ernie's girl and her brother were invited, too, and when they came, said they could smell that good dressing clear out in the yard. The hens practically plopped open in the pans and mamma's mashed potatoes and chicken gravy melted in the mouth. Oh, never did anyone have a nicer Christmas than the Kurtzes down on Mill Street.

It was when they were finishing Carrie's thick mince pies that the radio news came on, and the announcement of the prizes. So they pulled back their chairs to listen, with the girls cautioning the menfolks, "Now stick to what your bet was last night and don't anybody cheat by changing."

The announcer introduced the committee head, who gave a too wordy talk about civic pride. Then the prizes:

"The third prize of ten dollars to Doctor Amos R. Scott, 1821 High View Drive." That was Santa-in-the-chimney. And while Ernie and his group groaned their disappointment that it was only the third, the others laughed at them for their poor bet.

"The second . . . twenty-five dollars . . . Mr. Ramsey E. Porter, 1484 High View Drive." The blue lights! With Carrie and Lillie wanting to know what the judges were thinking of, for Pete's sake, to give it only second, and mamma and Ernie's girl calling out jubilantly that it left only their own choice, the reindeer.

Then a strange thing happened.

"Listen, everybody."

"Sh! What's he saying?"

"The first price . . . for its simplicity . . . for using materials at hand without expense . . . for its sacred note and the fact that it is the personification of the real Christmas story of which we sometimes lose sight . . . the first prize of fifty dollars is unanimously awarded to Mr. Harm Kurtz at 623 Mill Street."

A bomb would have torn fissures in the yard and made an unmendable shambles of the house, but it could not have been more devastating.

For a long moment they sat stunned, mouths open, but without speech coming forth, and only the little boys saying: "He said you, grandpa; he said you."

Then the hypnotic spell broke and Ernie let out a yell: "Fifty bucks, pa! Fifty bucks!"

And mamma, still dazed, kept repeating like some mournful raven, "But I just did it for the little boys."

Several got up and dashed over to the window to see again this first-prize paragon. But all they could see was Bird and Bell and the cow out in their little yard, an old dilapidated shed, and high up over it a piece of yellow glass.

In the midst of the excitement pa practically turned pale. For it had come to him suddenly there was more to this than met the eye. What would the Scotts and the Porters and the Dillinghams say? Especially Mr. Dillingham, whose expensive reindeer had won no prize at all. He was embarrassed and worried. The joy had gone out of winning the prize. The joy had gone out of the day.

The girls had scarcely finished the dishes before the Mill Street neighbors started coming to have a share in the big news. The Danish Hansens came and the Russian family from the next block, all three of the Czech families down the street, and the Negro children who lived near the mill. They were all alike to mamma. "Just folks." She made coffee and gave everyone a doughnut. In fact, they ate so many, that late in the afternoon she whipped up another batch. Also, out of honor to the great occasion, she combed her hair again in that high skinned-up way and put on a second clean apron. Two clean aprons in one day constituted the height of something or other.

"Somebody might come by," she said by way of apology.

"They'll get stuck in the mud if they do," said Ernie. "I'm the only one that knows them holes like a map."

Mamma was right. Somebody came by. All River City came by.

Soon after dusk, with the star lighted and Bird and Bell back in the shed, the cars began to drive past in unending parade. Traffic was as thick as it had ever been up on Main and Washington. You could hear talk and laughter and maybe strong words about the mud holes. Then in the front yard, both the talk and the laughter would die down, and there would be only low-spoken words or silence. Bird and Bell pulling at the hay. The cow gazing moodily into space. The pigeons on the ridgepole in a long feathery group. White Mary bending over a faint glow in the manger. And overhead the star.

In silence the cars would drive away and more come to take their places.

Three of them did not drive away. They swung in closer to the fence and all the people got out and came into the yard. Of all things!

"Mamma, there come the Scotts and the Porters and the Dillinghams." Pa was too excited for words and hardly knew what he was doing.

But mamma was cool and went out to meet them. "Sh! They're just folks too."

The Scotts were lifting the wheeled chair out of the car, which had been custom built for it. Doctor Scott wheeled the little boy up closer so he could see the animals. Carrie's little boys ran up to him and with the tactlessness of children showed him how they could turn cartwheels all around his chair.

"Why, Mr. Kurtz," Mrs. Porter was saying, "you're the sly one. Helping us all the time and then copping out the prize yourself."

Pa let it go. They would just have to believe it was all his doings, but for a fleeting moment he saw himself yanking madly at the shed boards.

Mrs. Her-I-don't-like Scott said, "It's the sweetest thing I ever saw. It made me feel like crying when I saw it."

Mrs. Dillingham said it made their decorations all look cheap and shoddy by the side of the manger scene. Even Mr. Dillingham, who had won no prize, said, "Kurtz, you certainly deserve it."

Pa knew he couldn't take any more praise. At least, not with mamma standing right there. So he said, "I guess it was mamma's idea. She's always gettin' ideas."

Right then mamma had another one. "Will you all please to step inside and have a cup of coffee and a doughnut?"

The women demurred, but all the men said they certainly would.

So they crowded into the kitchen, mink coats and all, and stood about with coffee and doughnuts. And Lillie got up her courage and said to Mr. Dillingham, "I don't suppose you know me, but I work for you."

"Oh, yes, sure; sure I do," he said heartily, but Lillie knew he was only being polite.

"And this is a friend of mine," she added with coy bravado, "Mr. Hansen."

Mr. Dillingham said, "How do you do, Mr. Hansen. Don't tell me you work for me too."

"Yes, sir, I do," said Lillie's new beau. "Packing."

And High View and Mill Street both laughed over it.

Mrs. Scott said, "Did you ever taste anything so good as these doughnuts? You couldn't find time to make me a batch once a week, could you?" So that Mrs. Dillingham and Mrs. Porter both said quickly, "Not unless she makes me one too."

And mamma, pleased as Punch, but playing hard to catch, said maybe she could.

Mr. Porter was saying to Ernie, "You folks ought to have some gravel down here on Mill Street."

And Ernie, who wasn't afraid of anyone, not even a councilman, said with infinite sarcasm, "You're telling me?"

The big cars all drove away. Three or four others straggled by. Then no more. And pa turned off the light of the star.

The house was still again except for the adenoidal breathing of one of the little boys. Even Ernie, coming in late, stopped tromping about upstairs. Everyone had to get up early to see Bert and Carrie off and get back to work. It made pa worry over his inability to get to sleep. This had been the most exciting day in years.

Mamma was lying quietly, her heavy body sagging down her side of the bed. It took all pa's self-control to pretend to sleep. Twice he heard the old kitchen clock strike another hour. He would try it.

"Mamma," he called softly.

"What?" she said instantly.

"Can't get to sleep."

"Wha's the matter?"

"Keep thinkin' of everything. All that money comin' to us. Company. Attention from so many folks. Children all home. Folks I work for all here and not a bit mad. You'd think I'd feel good. But I don't. Somethin' hangs over me. Like they'd been somebody real out there in the shed all this time; like we'd been leavin' 'em stay out when we ought to had 'em come on in. Fool notion—but keeps botherin' me."

And then mamma gave her answer. Comforting, too, just as he knew it would be. "I got the same feelin'. I guess people's been like that ever since it happened. Their conscience always hurtin' 'em a little because there wa'n't *no room for Him in the inn.*"